The Case of the
Great Sled Race

Read all the Jigsaw Jones Mysteries

Coming Soon

The Case of the Great Sled Race

by James Preller
illustrated by John Speirs
cover illustration by R. W. Alley

A
LITTLE APPLE
PAPERBACK

SCHOLASTIC INC.
New York   Toronto   London   Auckland   Sydney
Mexico City   New Delhi   Hong Kong

For Gavin

Book design by Dawn Adelman

ISBN 0-439-11427-6

Excerpts from *Stone Fox* by John Reynolds Gardiner © 1980. Reprinted with permission of HarperCollins Children's Books.

24   8 9/0

Printed in the U.S.A.   40
First Scholastic printing, January 2000

CONTENTS

Chapter One

Postcard from Florida

I sat at the kitchen table on a Sunday afternoon, warming my hands around a cup of hot chocolate. My toes were wet and cold. My nose was as red as Superman's cape. I was frozen solid, like a human Popsicle. It was the middle of January, and it had been snowing all weekend.

I glanced at the postcard on the table. It showed a white sandy beach, a green ocean, and a neat row of palm trees. Yellow letters floated across a blue sky: LIFE'S A BEACH!

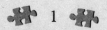

It was a perfect picture of a summer day. Only it wasn't summer. It was Miami. I flipped the card over. It read, *Weather is here. Wish you were wonderful.* That was Aunt Harriet's sense of humor, all right.

Yeesh.

Aunt Harriet was on vacation in Florida. She hated winter. Aunt Harriet complained about the cold, the mittens, the snow, the slush, the whole frozen mess.

Go figure.

Me? I'll take the four seasons anytime: spring, summer, fall, *and* winter. I always have two words for Aunt Harriet:

Snow.

Day.

What could be better? You wake up under thick, warm blankets. Your mom comes into the room and says, "Don't get up. It's a snow day. School's closed."

So the first thing you do is jump out of bed. No classes, no books, no homework.

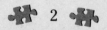

It's like a mini-vacation. A day for sled rides and snowball fights.

I glanced out the window, saw the fat white flakes drifting from the clouds, and flicked the postcard onto the table. Nope, they didn't have snow days in Florida. I'd have to remind Aunt Harriet next time I saw her.

I gobbled up my grilled cheese sandwich and hustled out the door. I could still get in a lot of sledding if I hurried. I was glad I didn't have any mysteries to solve. I mean, sure, I *loved* being a second-grade detective. And I made good money solving mysteries. But today I was taking the day off. Even a detective needs a break once in a while.

I was dragging my sled into the park when I spotted Bigs Maloney. Bigs was the roughest, toughest kid in second grade — but not taller than a grizzly bear and not

wider than a soda machine. He was headed my way.

Bigs stared straight ahead, mumbling to himself. He stopped in front of me. "Velma," he said. "I want my Velma back. You have to help me find her, Jigsaw."

Bigs put his giant paw on my shoulder.

And squeezed.

"Lay off the shoulder, will you?" I pleaded. "I might need that arm someday."

Bigs let go of my arm. He stared off into the distance. "I just want my Velma back," he said. "You have to help me."

Chapter Two

The Velocity Machine 2000

I led Bigs Maloney into my basement. I sat at my desk. Bigs sat across from me. I watched his gaze dance around the room. His eyes finally rested on the sign behind me.

JIGSAW JONES, PRIVATE EYE

"Grape juice?" I offered Bigs.

Bigs growled like a big dog. He said he didn't want any lousy grape juice.

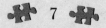

I shrugged and poured myself a glass.

"So who's Velma?" I asked.

Bigs gave me a strange look, as if a toucan had just landed on my hat.

"Velma," I repeated, speaking slowly. "Who is she?"

"Velma?" Bigs echoed.

Bigs was pretty shaken up. "Snap out of it, Bigs," I demanded. "What happened out there?"

Bigs glared darkly. I watched his thick fingers curl into fists. "Somebody stole my Velma," Bigs barked. "And you're gonna help me find the crumb who did it."

I ran my fingers through my hair. We'd been together for nearly twenty minutes, and I still didn't know what he was talking about. "Sit here," I told Bigs. "And don't chew on the furniture while I'm gone."

I took the stairs two at a time. Mila answered her phone on the third ring. "I'll be right over," she said.

Five minutes later, Mila was throwing questions at Bigs Maloney. "Who is this Velma you're talking about?" Mila asked. "I thought you liked Lucy Hiller?"

Bigs made a face, like he was disappointed in us. "Velma is a *what*, not a *who*," he said.

"What kind of *what*?" Mila asked.

"A *sled* kind of what — that's who!" Bigs shot back. "My Velocity Machine 2000. The fastest sled in town."

Finally I understood. *Vel*-ocity . . . *Ma*–chine. *Vel-ma*.

"Oh," I said. "Velma is the name of your sled!"

Bigs sneered. "And I'm gonna clobber the crumb who stole her."

Mila gave me a worried look.

Yeesh.

"Listen, Bigs," I said. "I don't think clobbering anybody is such a great idea.

But we'll help you find your sled. You know our rates. We get a dollar a day."

Bigs dug into his front pockets. He pulled out a fistful of soggy dollar bills. He peeled one from the crumpled mess and plastered it on my office desk. George Washington stared up at me.

I picked up the dollar bill and reached out my free hand. "It's a deal." We shook hands.

Mila cleared her throat. "This is all very nice," she said. "But we don't have any clues yet." Mila stared hard into Bigs Maloney's eyes. "Let's hear it, Bigs. Nice and slow. From the beginning. What happened to Velma?"

Chapter Three

The Crime Scene

"Follow me," Bigs answered.

We trudged through the snow. We headed for Lincoln Park, the scene of the crime. It was just a few blocks from my house. When it snowed, Long Hill was the most popular sledding spot in the park. There was a boathouse at the bottom of the hill, where you could rent paddleboats during the summer. In winter, they opened up the building for sledders. People came in to sit around the fire, eat curly french fries, and drink hot chocolate.

"Where'd you see Velma last?" I asked Bigs.

Bigs pointed to a spot beside the boathouse. There were ten or so sleds scattered on a snowbank. "I went inside for a Snickers bar," he said. "I left Velma right here, leaning against the wall. When I came back, she was gone."

"How long were you inside?" Mila asked.

"Ten minutes, maybe fifteen," Bigs said.

"Were you alone?" I asked.

"Yeah, alone," Bigs shot back, his face turning red. "Some bum took my Velma!" Bigs put his hands on his hips and growled. I half expected hot lava to pour from his ears. Bigs stomped around in circles. He packed a fat snowball. Then Bigs whirled and fired. The sun had to duck to get out of the way.

"Nice throw. Feel better now?" I asked.

"Nah," he snarled. "I'll only feel better when I get Velma back." Bigs stepped

forward, towering over me. I stared into his neck. Then I felt a brick crash down on my shoulder. Only it wasn't a brick. It was Bigs Maloney's hand.

"I want that sled back, Jigsaw," Bigs said between clenched teeth. "It's your job to get it back — or else."

Bigs turned and marched toward the hill.

"Or else?" I whispered to Mila. *Or else what?!* What do you think he means, *or else?*"

Mila just blinked. "I don't know exactly," she said. "But I think it would involve pain."

We caught up with Bigs at the base of the hill. He was watching the sledders race down the slope. His eyes looked moist. I was worried the big lug might burst into tears. Either that, or rip a tree out of the ground.

The hill was crowded with kids. They roared down the hill, screaming happily. A group of parents stood on the ridge. They stamped their feet on the ground, trying to stay warm. Some of them held camcorders. Parents, yeesh. They'll videotape *anything* — baseball games, Halloween parades, birthday parties, the works.

"Look at this," Mila said. She shoved a sheet of paper under my eyes.

Sign up today for...

JIMMY'S SPORTS EMPORIUM'S
2nd ANNUAL SLEDDING CONTEST
January 23. 1:00 P.M.
Singles and Doubles Races.
First Prize: Free Ice-skating Lessons!

"Did you know about this?" I asked Bigs.

"Sure, I knew about it," he answered. "What do you think I was doing here all day — collecting daisies? The races are in one week. And I was gonna win, too. Me and Velma. Nobody could beat us."

Mila and I locked eyes. It was our first clue. We left Bigs a few minutes later. On the way home, I talked over the case with my partner. "Maybe that's why the thief stole Velma," I suggested. "He knew Bigs would win the race."

"He or *she* knew," Mila corrected. "We don't know if the thief is a boy or a girl."

I shrugged. "So he, *or she,* steals the sled. That way Bigs can't be in the race. And the thief has a better chance to win."

"I'll get a list of everyone who signed up for the race," Mila said. "They're all suspects."

Chapter Four
Who, What, Where, When, and Why

The snow stopped falling around dinnertime. My parents seemed relieved. "It looks like you'll be going to school tomorrow," my father happily announced.

My brothers groaned. My sister, Hillary, angrily stabbed at her potatoes. Grams asked me what I'd been learning in school.

"Nothing," I explained.

"Reading any books?" she asked.

"We started one in class last week," I told her. "We're about halfway finished. It's called *Stone Fox* by John . . . Reynolds . . .

Gardiner." I told Grams the story. It was about a boy named Willy. He had a dog, Searchlight. They were just about to enter a dogsled race. Willy had to win or else he'd lose the family farm.

"Sounds good," Grams said.

I told her it wasn't good. "It's *great*."

After dinner, I pulled out my detective journal. I drew a picture of Bigs Maloney. It came out looking like Frankenstein on a bad hair day. In other words, it looked just like Bigs.

BIGS

I wrote: **THE CASE OF THE GREAT SLED RACE.**

I thought about the type of person who would steal a sled from Bigs Maloney. The thief would have to be brave, big, and tough. And more than a little crazy. Only a nut would mess with Bigs Maloney. It was my job to find the thief. And then, if I could, to stop Bigs from ripping off the poor guy's arms and legs.

I crawled into bed, dead tired. Maybe it would start snowing again. Maybe tomorrow would be a snow day.

Hey, a guy can dream, can't he?

First thing in the morning, I looked out my bedroom window. The sky was sunny

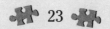

and clear. The white snow, reflecting the sun, stung my eyes. There was a knock at the door.

"Up and at 'em, kiddo," my dad gleefully called. "It's not snowing and the roads are open. Better get dressed for school."

Yeesh.

My class is in room 201. Ms. Gleason is the best teacher in the whole school, easy. She's tall and she smiles a lot. In reading circle, we read chapter seven of *Stone Fox.* Ms. Gleason read out loud:

Little Willy needed his rest. So did Searchlight. Tomorrow was going to be a big day. The biggest day of their lives.

Ms. Gleason closed the book. "Tomorrow we'll read chapter eight," she announced.

We all groaned. "Can't you keep reading?" begged Helen Zuckerman.

"Please!" chimed in Joey Pignattano.

"Pretty please," said Ralphie Jordan. "We'll be good all day — even if it kills us!"

Ms. Gleason smiled. "Mr. Gardiner is a terrific writer. But we've got a lot of other work to do." She walked over to the blackboard. Ms. Gleason said, "As you know, we should always be *thinking* while we're reading. That's how we *understand* what's happening in the story. Today I'd like to talk about a few strategies that will help us *think* about what we're reading."

Ms. Gleason told us about *The Five "W" Questions*. Who, what, where, when, and why. She pulled out a big chart and we brainstormed together. The *Who* questions told us about characters. *Where* and *When* told us about the book's setting. *Why* and *What* told about the story, or plot.

I suddenly realized it was like solving a mystery. Reading was like detective work. Figure out the *W* questions . . . and you'll catch the crook.

Chapter Five
Breaking the Code

I found a note in my desk after lunch:

Blue the breezy I'm frog rice rainy getting
fat cat sunny the song freezing list sled
cloudy tonight.

I recognized Mila's handwriting. It was in code. Mila was always testing my brainpower. I studied the note carefully. Then I noticed a pattern. The note used a lot of weather words. *Breezy, rainy, sunny, freezing,* and *cloudy.* We'd just started a weather unit in school. So I knew all about that stuff.

I remembered another code we used. It was a color code. The only words that mattered were the ones that came right after a color word. Maybe this was the same. I circled *breezy, rainy, sunny, freezing,* and *cloudy.* Then I underlined the words that were next.

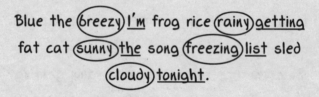

The message read:

I'm getting the list tonight.

Mila was probably going to Jimmy's Sports Emporium. All she had to do was find out who had signed up for the same race as Bigs Maloney. I made eye contact with Mila. I slid my finger across my nose. That was our secret signal. It meant I got the message.

In the afternoon, Ms. Gleason made us answer *W* questions. They were about *Stone Fox*. Ms. Gleason wrote sentences on the blackboard. Then we had to decide if the underlined words told *who, what, when,* or *where.* I wrote down my answers.

Where	1.	Little Willy lived <u>in Wyoming</u>.
When	2.	Grandfather laid in bed for <u>weeks</u>.
What	3.	Searchlight pulled <u>the sled</u>.
Who	4.	<u>Stone Fox</u> never lost a race.

Ms. Gleason gave us ten sentences in all. And you know what? It was just like detective work. I pulled out my journal and scribbled some notes:

WHAT	Velma = Bigs Maloney's sled
WHERE	Long Hill
WHEN	Jan. 16
WHY	Win the race?
WHO	? ? ?

In the detective business, there's another word for "why." It's called *motive*. When you try to guess a criminal's motive, you are really asking *why* they did

something. For instance: Why does someone rob a bank? To get rich. That's the *motive*.

But why steal Bigs Maloney's sled? Mila and I could only guess. We didn't know for sure. Not yet, anyway. Someone probably stole the sled because they wanted to win the race.

One thing was for sure. I wouldn't want to be the thief. Because sooner or later, we'd catch him (or her). We always did. And then he (or she) would have to answer to Bigs Maloney.

Chapter Six

Mila Comes Through

"I've got some bad news, Jigsaw."

It was Mila on the phone.

"You couldn't get the list?" I guessed.

"No, I got the list all right," Mila said. "But we've got our work cut out for us. A lot of kids signed up for that race."

"Do we know any of them?" I asked.

"Sure," Mila answered. "All of 'em. I signed you up, too."

"You what?"

"I signed you up," Mila said. "I had to — that's how I got to see the list. I thought it would seem weird if I just *looked* at the list. So I signed you up. You're in the singles race, ages six to eight. One o'clock on Sunday."

Yeesh. I didn't exactly love the idea of racing against Bigs Maloney. I'd rather go swimming with Orca the Killer Whale.

Mila read the names to me over the phone. I jotted them down in my journal:

Bigs Maloney   Joey Pignattano
Lucy Hiller   Jasper Noonan
Ralphie Jordan   Wingnut O'Brien
Bobby Solofsky   Nicole Rodriguez
Mike Radcliffe   Jigsaw Jones

"Not counting me and Bigs, that makes eight suspects," I said.

I could almost hear Mila nod in agreement.

"Hey, Mila," I said. "Fluff up my memory. Who's Jasper Noonan?"

He's all talk, anyway. I kept right on sledding."

Later on, I managed to talk with Mike Radcliffe and Bobby Solofsky. They said the same thing as Nicole: Bigs Maloney made a big fuss up on the hill. I frowned at the news. That meant the thief was probably scared. Now he'd *really* be hard to find.

When I got back to room 201, I had a surprise waiting for me. But she wasn't wrapped in a bow.

Chapter Seven
Detective Work

Lucy Hiller had curly hair, red boots, a bright purple skirt, and a missing front tooth. She was leaning on my desk when I returned from lunch.

"Can we talk?" she asked.

"We *are* talking," I replied.

"Not here," she said. Lucy pulled on my shirt. "In private. It's about the case."

"Watch the shirt," I complained. "It's a family heirloom."

Lucy looked puzzled.

"A hand-me-down," I explained.

Suddenly, Lucy's eyes widened. I followed her gaze to see a group of kids enter the room. Bigs Maloney was with them. "I'll call you," Lucy whispered. "Tonight."

Lucy hurried back to her seat. I stood there scratching the back of my neck. Why would Lucy Hiller be afraid of Bigs Maloney?

Ms. Gleason read chapter eight of *Stone Fox*. We listened in perfect silence. Everyone was dying to find out what happened next. In the story, the townspeople had gathered to watch the race. But no one thought little Willy could win — except maybe Searchlight, Willy, Doc Smith, and me.

Ms. Gleason read, "*'Mayor Smiley raised a pistol to the sky and fired. The race had begun!'*"

Then she closed the book. "That's all for today."

"What?!" squealed Helen Zuckerman. "You can't stop reading *now*!"

"I'm sorry," Ms. Gleason said. "It's the end of the chapter."

Yeesh. We were all mad at the author. It wasn't fair to end the chapter right in the middle of the action. Ms. Gleason laughed and said it was called a *cliffhanger*. She said, "The author wants to keep you on the edge of your seats. He wants you to hurry up to the next chapter."

Bobby Solofsky said it was a dirty, rotten trick.

"Perhaps," Ms. Gleason replied. "But it works!"

I sat next to Mila on the bus ride home. Mila told me she had talked to two suspects — Ralphie Jordan and Lucy Hiller.

"Anything turn up?" I asked.

"Not exactly," Mila said. "But Lucy seemed . . ."

". . . interested?" I said, finishing her sentence.

Mila's eyes shifted toward me. "Yes, very interested," she said. "Lucy wanted to know *everything* about the case."

"Did you find that odd?" I asked.

"Not really," Mila replied. "I mean, Lucy has always liked Bigs Maloney. I figure she just cares a lot."

I didn't say anything. Maybe that was it.

Maybe Lucy just cared a lot.

Maybe.

But then again, maybe aardvarks played hopscotch on Tuesday nights. I didn't like *maybes*. I wanted facts.

We had doorbells to ring. Wingnut O'Brien was first, because he lived next door to me. We called him Wingnut on account of his ears. They were three sizes too big for his head.

Wingnut said he left Long Hill early on Sunday. "I signed up for the race. Then I went to Freddy Fenderbank's birthday party," he explained.

We shoved on. Nobody was home at Joey Pignattano's. We hit Stringbean's house. Mila knew where he lived. "He's neighbors with Lucy Hiller," she told me.

Jasper Noonan was surprised to see us. I mean, he practically *fainted*. I suppose he wasn't used to having visitors. Jasper didn't even invite us in. Instead, he held the door open a crack and poked his head out. He coughed and sneezed a lot. "I'b all snuffed up," Jasper said. He wiped his nose with his sleeve. Gross me out the door.

Jasper said he was at Long Hill on Sunday. But he didn't see anybody take Velma.

"Were you alone?" Mila asked.

Jasper's eyes flickered. "Yeth," he answered. "Why? Do you tink I stole it?"

I waved the thought away. "No, Jasper. We're just asking a few questions. Thanks for your help." Mila and I turned to leave.

"Is Bigs still . . . mad?" Jasper asked.

We stopped in our tracks.

"Bigs seebed really mad . . . up on the hill," Jasper said through his stuffed-up nose. "He said id was clobbering tibe."

Clobbering time. I forced a smile. "That's Bigs Maloney for you."

"Do you thik he would really . . . clobber . . . sobebody?" Jasper asked.

A sudden wind crept up. Jasper shivered.

"Yes," I answered. "Bigs would."

Jasper's face turned white. His eyes grew watery. Then he sneezed hard enough to knock the glasses off his nose.

Poor guy.

He sure caught a bad cold.

At least I *think* it was a cold.

Anyway, it was a bad case of something.

Chapter Eight

A Call from Lucy

After our visit with Stringbean, it was time to get home. So we did. It gets dark early in January. Mila and I didn't have much to say about the case. We both knew we needed another clue. We talked about *Stone Fox* instead. Mila said it was a great work of *literature.* That's Mila for you. Sometimes she likes to use grown-up words. I don't hold it against her. I told Mila that *Stone Fox* was the best work of literature I'd read since *Captain Underpants and the Attack of the Talking Toilets.*

Mila rolled her eyes.

Go figure.

I was working on my homework when the phone rang. It was Lucy Hiller.

"Hi, Lucy." I wondered what she wanted. "What do you want?" I asked.

"Um, like, nothing," she said.

"Oh," I answered. "Well, bye. I guess I'll talk to you later."

"Wait!" she said.

I waited. Finally I said, "Look, Lucy. You called because you wanted to tell me something. So go ahead. Tell me something."

Lucy took a deep breath. "Um, like, I was wondering how the case was going. Any suspects?"

"A few," I lied.

"Anyone I know?" she asked.

The question floated by like a bubble. I didn't pop it. Lucy asked a few more questions about the sled. I answered most

of them with a shrug. On the phone, that's not real helpful. But then again, I wasn't trying to be helpful. I had a picture of George Washington in my pocket that said I was working for Bigs Maloney. Not Lucy Hiller.

"Why do *you* care so much?" I asked her.

"No reason," Lucy said. "Just curious."

I sure was. I hung up the phone and wrote in my journal:

WHY IS LUCY SO CURIOUS?
DID SHE STEAL THE SLED?

Next morning, I caught up with Joey Pignattano at the bus stop. In the detective business, you learn a lot about people. Sometimes one small fact will tell you a lot about a guy. For example: Joey Pignattano once ate a live, wriggling worm for a dollar. That's about all you need to know about Joey Pignattano. He was a worm-eating kind of guy. But I liked him anyway. He always seemed like an honest person.

Still, there was the problem of a missing sled named Velma.

I had to keep asking questions. Sooner or later somebody would come up with an answer I liked.

"I didn't do it!" Joey told me. "And I can prove it!"

"Prove it?" I asked. "How?"

"My parents were there the whole time. They can vouch for me," Joey said.

I stamped my feet to keep out the cold. I remembered all the parents on top of Long Hill. I remembered . . . camcorders. "By any chance, were your parents making a video?"

Joey beamed. "How did you guess that?"

"Dumb luck," I said. "Can I watch it?"

Joey shrugged. "I guess so. Why?"

"Why?" I repeated. "*Why?!* I'm not sure, Joey. I'm still working on who, what, when, and where."

Chapter Nine
The Video Clue!

I couldn't wait for the school day to end. I wanted to get to Joey's house and watch that video. I had a feeling that it might hold a clue that could break the case wide open. Meanwhile, I was trapped in school. But the day wasn't all bad. Ms. Gleason read the last two chapters of *Stone Fox*. The ending was happy *and* sad. I noticed that even Bigs Maloney cried a little.

That was a mistake.

Because Bigs *noticed* that *I* noticed. A few minutes later, he came over to my desk.

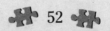

Bigs jabbed a finger into my chest. *Ping*. It felt like an aluminum baseball bat. "I paid you," he said. "Now I want my Velma back."

"Easy on the chest, will you, Bigs? I store my heart in there."

Bigs frowned.

Ping. He jabbed me again.

Mila stepped between us. "We've just about solved the case, Bigs! You'll have Velma back by tomorrow!" she promised.

"Really?" Bigs asked.

Mila gave Bigs her biggest smile. "Really," she said. I noticed that her fingers were crossed behind her back.

An enormous grin filled Bigs Maloney's face. He was suddenly as happy as a puppy with a new chew toy. *Whack!* His giant hand slapped my back. My eyeballs nearly rolled across the floor. "Thanks a lot, you guys!" Bigs shouted. "Thanks a million! Thanks a . . . thanks . . . a . . . *gazillion!*" Then he walked away. I mean, *maybe* he walked. I don't know for sure. The big lug was so happy he might have floated away on fluffy white clouds.

I looked at Mila. She shrugged back at me. "I had to tell him something," she explained.

"I guess," I said.

"Bigs is a little rough," Mila observed.

"Yeah, I noticed," I said, rubbing my chest. "But it's not easy losing something

you love. Even if it's only a sled. Remember when I lost Rags?"

Mila remembered. How could she forget? I was a total mess. My dog was lost for three whole days.

"I think that's how Bigs feels right now," I said. "The big hockey puck doesn't know what to do. I feel sorry for the guy. Bigs talks tough. But have you ever *seen* him actually hurt anybody?"

Mila thought it over. "Come to think of it, no."

"See," I said. "Bigs doesn't really *want* to clobber anybody. It's like he says. He just wants his Velma back."

We rushed over to Joey's house after school. Mila even brought a bag of popcorn for everyone to share. Oh, brother. It wasn't like we were watching Nickelodeon. This was a home movie of Joey Pignattano rolling around in the snow.

And making goofy faces.

And sledding down the hill.

And walking up the hill.

And picking his nose.

And sledding down the hill. Then up again. Then down. Up. Down. Up.

After half an hour, I asked Joey, "Exactly how long *is* this video?"

He told me it was almost over.

I hoped he was right.

The movie played on. Meanwhile, I tried to decide which was worse: watching

Joey's home movie . . . or having a tooth pulled.

With rusty pliers.

I was still trying to decide when something caught my eye. "Stop the tape," I demanded.

Joey stopped the tape.

"Rewind."

Joey rewound the tape.

"There!" I said. "Stop right there."

Joey pressed the pause button. I stared at the picture for a solid minute.

I clicked off the television. "We've got 'em."

Chapter Ten

In Jasper's Room

I placed a phone call to Lucy Hiller. I told her we were on our way to Jasper Noonan's house. I told Lucy that I knew Jasper stole the sled. I also told her that Bigs was going to clobber him.

I wasn't exactly telling the truth.

I waited about half an hour before doing push-ups on Jasper's doorbell.

Jasper answered the door. He looked at me and Mila. Jasper peered behind us — and to the sides. It was like he was looking for Bigs Maloney.

And he was.

I was sure that Lucy had already gotten to him.

"It's just us," I said. "Let's talk."

Jasper swallowed hard. He led me and Mila into his bedroom. It looked more like a planetarium. The room was painted black. It had stars and planets painted on the ceiling and walls. It was weird . . . and strange . . . and totally cool.

"Wow," I said.

"Spacey," Mila observed.

Jasper just stood by, fidgeting nervously.

"I think you know why we're here, Stringbean." I told him it was time for the truth.

Jasper sat down on the bed. He held his head in his hands. He finally stared up at me. He was trying to decide something.

Could he trust me . . . or not?

"Let's just *suppose* somebody took the

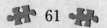

sled," Jasper finally said. He didn't quite look me in the eye.

"Sure, Jasper," I said. "We could play it that way. Let's suppose."

"And let's *suppose*," he continued, "that this *person* only meant to borrow it."

I nodded. "Keep talking, Jasper."

"Bigs was mad when he couldn't find his sled," Jasper said. "*Real* mad. I'd bet the

person who borrowed the sled might be afraid to return it."

I didn't bite. But I saw the worm on the hook. "So?" I said.

"So," Jasper echoed. "Just suppose somebody still *had* the sled. Even if he *wanted* to return it, maybe he'd be afraid to — because Bigs would pound him into dust."

I took the bait. "You wouldn't happen to *be* this person, would you, Jasper?"

Jasper looked down. He bit his lip. He untucked his shirt and tucked it back in again. "No, I mean, of course not. I was just supposing."

Oh, brother.

"Well, let's suppose this," I said. "Let's suppose I get Bigs Maloney over here. Let's suppose I tell Bigs that you stole Velma. What do you *suppose* Bigs Maloney might do?"

Jasper turned pale. He started to stammer.

"That's enough, Jigsaw!"

The voice came from behind the closet door.

Lucy Hiller stepped out.

"Don't look so surprised," she told me. "I've been hiding here all the time."

"I'm *not* surprised," I answered. "In fact, I was counting on it."

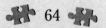

It was Lucy's turn to look surprised.

I continued, "That's why I called you first, Lucy. I knew you were in on it with Jasper." I held up the videotape. "Joey's parents like to make home movies," I explained. "Boring stuff, most of it. Except for one little scene. A scene that stars Jasper — and you, Lucy. Remember? It was last Sunday afternoon. Near Long Hill. When you two went off with Bigs Maloney's Velocity Machine 2000."

Lucy started to argue. "But . . ."

I held up my hand. "It's all on tape. There's no use denying the facts. I know *who,* and *what,* and *when,* and *where.* But I don't know *why.*"

I paused. "So finish the puzzle for me," I said. *"Why did you take Bigs Maloney's sled?"*

Chapter Eleven
The Great Sled Race

"I knew you'd make trouble, Jigsaw," Lucy muttered. "The minute Bigs hired you, I knew you'd make trouble."

"I'm a detective," I replied. "Trouble is my business."

Lucy put a hand on Jasper's shoulder. "I'm sorry, Stringbean," she said. "I can't protect you anymore."

Jasper looked like a sick puppy. If he had a tail, it would have been between his legs.

"I don't get it," Mila said. "Why did you steal the sled, Lucy?"

Lucy shook her head. "Nobody *stole* the sled," she answered. "Stringbean only borrowed it without asking, sort of."

Jasper sniffed and looked up at Lucy. He spoke up. "I just wanted to try it. Just once. It looked so cool."

A lightbulb went off over my head. I saw it all clearly. "But Bigs noticed the sled was gone before you could return it," I said. "He started making threats . . ."

". . . and I got scared," Jasper confessed. "I hid the sled in the bushes."

It was Lucy's turn to talk. "I saw what happened," she admitted. "I've been neighbors with Stringbean all my life. He's not a thief. I didn't want Bigs to hurt him. So I helped Jasper hide the sled."

She looked at Mila, then at me. Right in the eye. "That's the truth."

I believed her.

"You still have the sled?" I asked.

Jasper nodded.

"I'll take it off your hands," I said. "But I won't tell Bigs where I got it. You don't have anything to be afraid of."

"But what if Bigs finds out?" Jasper asked.

"Don't worry," I answered. "I'll handle Bigs Maloney. He just wants his sled back."

* * * * *

It was the day of the big race. So we all piled on the layers — long underwear and itchy sweaters — and climbed Long Hill.

Mila towed a sled, too. Of course, Mila hadn't mentioned that she signed us up for the doubles race, too. "Let's win," she said. "Why not?"

I smiled at her through my scarf. "Why not!"

The Velocity Machine 2000 lived up to expectations. Bigs easily won the singles race. Ralphie Jordan came in second. Bigs

never suspected a thing. He had his Velma back — it was all that mattered. He really wasn't the clobbering type.

Who won the doubles race?

Well, with a partner like Mila . . . how could a guy lose?

Afterward we all went inside for curly fries and hot chocolates. Joey Pignattano's parents made a video of the whole thing. I was happy with the way things turned out.

Bigs got his sled back.

Mila and I won free skating lessons.

And nobody got hurt.

Hey, what did you expect? They don't call me the best detective in second grade for nothing!

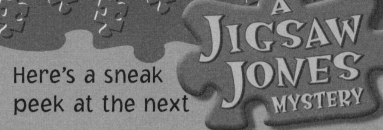

Here's a sneak peek at the next **A JIGSAW JONES MYSTERY**

The Case of the Stinky Science Project

by James Preller

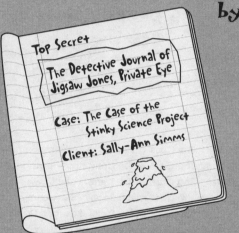

Top Secret

The Detective Journal of Jigsaw Jones, Private Eye

Case: The Case of the Stinky Science Project

Client: Sally-Ann Simms

Bobby Solofsky fooled Sally-Ann with a phony magic trick. It was a rotten trick. But that's not all that stinks. Something smelly is spoiling science time in Ms. Gleason's class. Could Bobby be the culprit? Jigsaw and Mila are hot on the case.

Coming Soon in March